the sleepy little alphabet

A Bedtime Story from Alphabet Town

written by **judy sierra** • illustrated by **melissa sweet**

SCHOLASTIC INC.

Ee Ff Gg Hh Ii

Nn Oo Pp Qq

Ww Xx Yy Zz

A is for Alden
—J.S.

To my three rascal friends—Grace, Lucy, and Georgia
—M.S.

ISBN 978-0-545-64638-3

Text copyright © 2009 by Judy Sierra.
Illustrations copyright © 2009 by Melissa Sweet.
All rights reserved. Published by Scholastic Inc., 557 Broadway, New York, NY 10012,
by arrangement with Alfred A. Knopf, an imprint of Random House Children's Books, a division of Random House, Inc.
SCHOLASTIC and associated logos are trademarks and/or registered trademarks of Scholastic Inc.

12 11 10 9 8 7 6 5 4 3 2 1   13 14 15 16 17 18/0

Printed in the U.S.A.   88

First Scholastic printing, September 2013

It's sleepytime in Alphabet Town.
As moms and dads run round and round,

the little letters skitter-scatter,
helter-skelter—what's the matter?

Uh-oh! **a** is wide awake.

And **b** still has a bath to take

with chubby **c**

and rub-a-dub **d**.

"Make room for me!" says eensy **e**.

f is full of fidgety wiggles.

g has got the googly giggles.

h tries standing on her head.

i and **j** jump on the bed.

h   i   j

k won't give a kiss good night.

l cries, "Don't turn off the light!"

m is mopey,

n is naughty.

Oops!

o and p upset the potty.

q is quiet as a bunny.

r and S read something funny.

t tucks in her teddy bear.

u takes off his underwear.

V is very, very snoozy.

W is wobbly-woozy.

x expects a great big hug.

y is a yawning cuddle bug.

Who's that snoring **Z z z**'s?

See you in the morning, abc's!

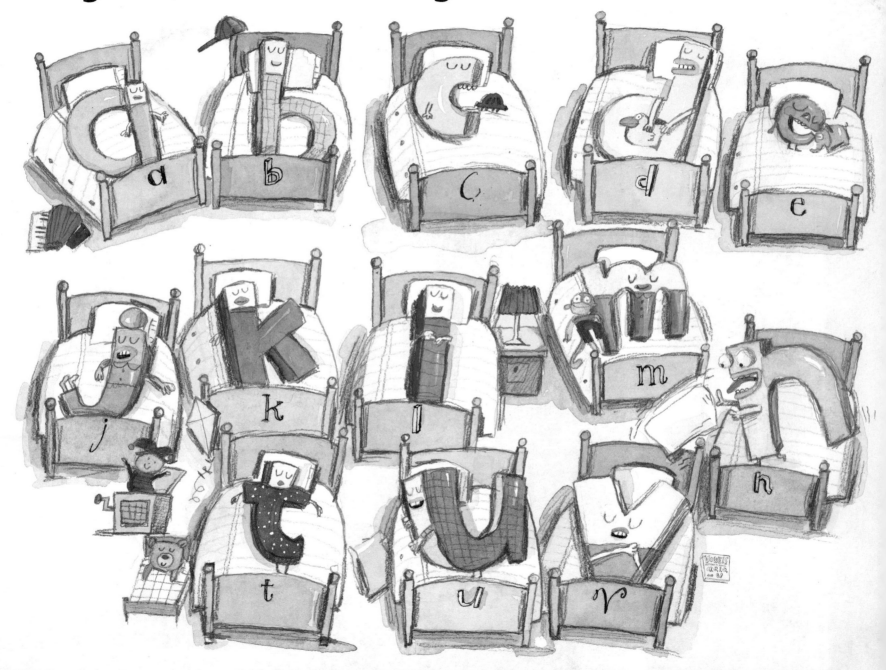

Aa Bb Cc Dd

Jj Kk Ll Mm

Rr Ss Tt Uu Vv